FUTURE REBUKE

By

Edward T. Tookes

PART I

My Narration: Today we are talking to boundaries and telling them to move.
On paper I'm not bound to time, space or any other issues.
So after acquiring of this new knowledge this is what we gone do.
I'm going to talk to my future self for a future rebuke.

Let's start right here right now in 2007.
I'm age 16 and I'm in the present.
Today I'm on my way to heaven.
But I need to make sure I got God in 2011.

By the end of that year I'll be 21.
I'll be old enough to smoke cigarettes and drink rum.
I know now that there's other ways to have fun.
But I might forget that in two-o-one-one.

Now how am I going to skip ahead in time?
I need to watch Hop in the Future on channel 9.
I sneak into the TV quiet as a mime.
Then I talk to Manny about borrowing his ride.
Manny I need that Crown Victorian even though it's not mine.

Manny: What are you doing with it going to fight crime?

Me: No, I need it to fix my future ahead of time.

Manny: Ok go ahead but there's some papers you have to sign.

My Narration: I show him my signature and I bust out of channel 9.

I get in the car and skip ahead 4 years.
Then I go to my future college where I live with my peers.
I go to my future dorm everybody's drinking beers.
There must be a party going on around here.
Then I see myself and I'm not looking in a mirror.
The only change is I'm taller with a mustache and a beard.
My future self and I find a place to hide.
He asked "How did you get here little guy?"
I grabbed his shoulder and said look me in the eye.
Remember these words until you and I both die.

Me: So you think you a grown up, cause you're 21!
Well I got news for you, you still ain't done.
For the rest of your life you will always be your father's son.
Don't get too involved with someone just because
you call her ya honey bun.

Having sex with someone outside of marriage is
like playing with a loaded gun.

If you fool around with it you might hurt someone.
And when you wind up with a kid then what huh?
You just gone pack ya bags take off and run.
Then you leave your girl carrying a baby for 9 months.
Kid grows up without a father, that's not fun.
"I hate men," that would become your baby mama's opinion.

So, be real is that what you want.

Then stop messin with someone you call your honey bun.

My Future Self: Hey little man that was real.
I understand where you coming from, I know how you feel.
But remember if I'm you and you're me then I'm the real deal.

Once you put your life in God's hands the covenant is sealed.
Jesus Christ is the only one who can really heal.
He won't charge, and leave you empty like a happy meal.
If you remember that, then you'll never lose ya zeal.

Me: Ok so if you're a Christian, what are you doing here?

My Future Self: I'm here to look out for my peers.
Somebody's got to keep the peace.
Anybody who drinks gives me their keys.

	This way there won't be any drunk drivers on the streets. If anybody needs a ride, they just come to me. But it ain't just parties that need somebody. It's the community the county and the whole society. That's why I'm running for president of this country.
Me:	Ok, I get it. Now I understand. You just don't want this thing to get out of hand. I'm glad somebody's finally taking a stand. Ya know what I think I'm your biggest fan. But my visit might interfere with ya future plans. So I'm going to hit you in the head with a frying pan.
	# BAM!!
	Now, you're out cold like a piece of ham. When you wake up you'll think you got hit by a mini van. Then you can still keep striving to be great man. Now that my work here is done let me get back to my Victorian.
My Narration:	So now I'm just relaxin and riding. I can fall asleep because my car is flying.

I got this car for a while and I'm not
buying.
I can travel to any time, hey I'm not
crying.
So I put the car on autopilot and I'm not
driving.
Then I pass out behind the wheel while
the car is still going.

My senses are turned off but the car is
still rolling.
I have a dream that my brother is driving
a car that's golden.
Then
Boom!!

A train hits the car that he rode in. My
brother dies because
his left door folded in. I wake up
thinking man I wish I could have told
him
he's more valuable to me than a million
gold tokens.
I'll always remember the words he's
spoken.
And how we used to be in church singing
those old hymns.
I would never want my brother to die
such a cold end.
Even though it's a dream it could be an
omen.
So I need to go to the future and show
him.
But I don't know how I'm gonna get
there cause my car got stolen.

Now I'm searching scanning looking for
a clue.
My car is gone, and I don't know what to
do.

If I don't find that thing then I'm in deep dodo.
My brother could die and Manny will be mad too.
I see a man in the distance, and I'm like who are you?

Arrabuu: Hello my American friend my name is Arrabuu.

Me: Arrabuu?

Arrabuu: I'm from India and I used to be a Guru.
I came to America because I wanted to buy new shoes.
So I flew here all the way from Jakapukoo
But the airport wouldn't let my camel through.
So they shipped it to a southern country called Puru.
If I don't get that camel he might catch the flu.
That American air will make him sick like A-Choo.

Me: Hey man, look dude I lost something too.
I had a dream my brother died and I wonder if it's true.
Then my car got stolen by someone I don't know who
if you help me then I'll help you.

I get the car you get ya camel out of Peru.
We gone fine something nice to do like Caillou.
We gone be tight cause we a two man crew.

Cause we gone hold together like the blue man group.
Come on Arrabuu I'm not gone hand hold you.
But we need to roll out like tomato can soup.

My Narration: A thug rolls up looking to hurt somebody.

Thug: He says "I'MA bust you up if you don't start riding."

Me: You can't bust me up man, I know karate.
Why you fronting like you want to come and rob me?
Me and my boy Arrabuu want no trouble obviously.
I see your boys in that car ready to pop me.
But you still need to wipe ya nose cause ya attitude is snotty.
I'm trying to save my brother and you trying to stop me.

You got another problem dog, and it's not me.
Somebody way back said you aint' hot B.
But don't listen to em, if you need a friend then you got me.
Why do I care about someone who wants to drop me?
Because I live my whole life trying to be Godly.
Now you still have ya gun just in case you want to pop me.

My Narration:	Then the thug has a gun in my face waiting to clock me. He throws down the gun looking big and stocky.
Thug:	I can't shoot a friend who tried to adopt me. If I killed you and Arrabuu I'd be like a bad cop see. Making innocent people die that's not my block B. So I'm not gonna shoot you just because somebody shot me.
My Narration:	I tell the thug we gotta go. And he's like "come back."
Thug:	I know you trying to look for ya brother and your car got jacked. I even know where it's at. I'm the one who stole the car matter fact.
My Narration:	Arrabuu's like"why did you go and do that?" The thug answers and says "He gave me a money filled sack."
Thug:	So I did it, and took your car like some kind of hood rat. When he found out whose car it was he sent me to attack. Soon after that he said he would pay me a stack.
My Narration:	So then I had to ask
Me:	Who put you up to this some computer hack?
Thug:	I don't know but he hides behind this chair that's all black.

	On top of that he wears some kind of face mask. He calls himself S.T.F. like he's some kind of Big Mac. But really he's so whack.
Me:	Ok so where do I go to get my car?
My Narration:	The thug says it's about 3 miles away. So it ain't that far.
Thug:	It's on some street that starts with an "R." River, Richard, or Rivet, or Revetwar. Whatever street it's not that hard if you see a big warehouse that's really, really large. Inside of there that's where your Crown Vic is parked. But be careful because that place is always watched by guards. Plus S.T.F. is in there making demands like a movie star. So good luck going in there and trying to find ya car.
Me:	Thanks man, for being who you are. I know you a thug but God knows you got heart. I gotta go, but our friendship is like a big cigar. We may be far apart but we still stick together like black tar. Now let's go Arrabuu. We gotta get that c-a-r.
My Narration:	Me and Arrabuu run to the warehouse. It was only 15 blocks. When I saw the size of it I was shocked.

I tried to open the door but whole thing
was locked.
Arrabuu tapped the door like knock
knock.
A guard opened the door and
we snuck in with a barrel full of rocks.

When we got in guards were
spread out like the Chicken Pox.
I saw a cube shaped room at the top.
I figured hey that's probably where
my car is stocked.

We turned off the lights and ran up the
back docks.

We got in the room we saw that was
shaped like box.
When I saw that big black chair I think
my heart stopped.
The chair turned slowly and it was
Sterling the canine jock.
I was laughing so hard I couldn't keep on
my socks.
I saw my car right next to the laundry
drop.

Yeah I do my laundry
in a warehouse too, … not.

Sterling starts to get out of his chair and
begins to hop.
He ran going for the car. I yell out you
better stop.

Me: You can't keep stealing stuff that ain't
yours like Goldie Locks.

Sterling no stealing.
Sterling no stealing.
Sterling no stealing.

My Narration: Me and Arrabuu jump in the car
and bust out of there quick as lightening.

Sterling made me laugh my socks off.
So I slip back on my Nikes.

Now that I got the car.
I gotta do the right thing like Spike Lee.
his time nobody's gonna try to fight me.
Lord don't let the devil try to come in
and hype me.
Guide me, and let my spirit shine
brightly
cause it don't matter what the world
thinks
as long as you still like me.

PART II

My Narration: Me and Arrabuu fly off to South America.
Arrabuu leanin out the window
like it ain't a chair in the caw.
When we land in Peru and it's like
letting a bear out the box.
When I open the door he's ready to
tear up the spot.

I hope it's not illegal to park a flying car
cause if I get it taken here
walking home is too far.
Then I'll be stuck here like
like cookies in a jar.
But Arrabuu seems to like
things the way they are.
Once he finds his camel
I'm hoppin out of here
like Kareem Abdul Jabar.

Wait a minute Arrabuu is that your camel?

Arrabuu: Yes it is, now I can finally rest.
Thank you for finding him you're the best.

Me: Don't mention it, glad it's off my chest.

My Narration: Now that I helped you I gotta continue my quest.
I gotta save my brother in North America so I'm
headed out west.

I get back in the car and switch it to
flying gear.
When the Crown Vic flies it's really hard
to steer.
So to find my brother I need a
destination
and a year.

In the dream he's in LA.
The train tracks what he's near.
But what happens next is what
I really fear.

Just thinking about it makes
me burst into tears.
My brother's life ends
during the screeching noise I hear.

The pain of my brother's death still burns
in my ear.
The train hits the car faster than a jet that
says lear.

So switch the car to #8
the time traveling gear.
In 2033 I arrive in LA
at a docking pier.
Now I can save my brother
before he disappears.

I hide my car behind the boat bow.
It's so cold outside you'd think we were
in Moscow.
But that's no matter cause this coat

makes me feel, look, and smell like a
cow.

Off the deck and into the streets
I'm a little hungry so I stop by
Mickey Dees.

I tell em never mind I don't want
a hamburger I want Japanese.
Everything is different in the 2030s.
So I gotta get new clothes so
the people won't tease.
People in this time got good technology
cars with swing up doors
and fold up TVs.
I get some new shoes, and try em on for
squeeze.
They're made of metal, with air holes in
em like Swiss cheese.

People like music when they run.
So the shoes play CDs.
I asked the clerk, hey sir how much.
He said they were about 7Gs.
Then he said you look like a nice kid.
I'll give em to you for free.

I walk out the store like
Ha ha ha hee hee.
I saved 7,000 on some shoes.
And I didn't pay a penny.

But yea the shoes are well.
The shoes are good.

But if I don't find my brother
the shoes are like firewood.

I'd use them once and burn em up

like a camper would.
So that's why I must save my brother
and return the shoes that I could
sell to a crook, but I won't cause
I must do as I should.

I could find my brother's address
and his life will be off the hook.
So I walk in a random store like
"look."

Me: My brother's about to die
and I need a phone book.

Store Owner: I'll sell it to ya if you clean
my counter every cranny every nook.
Why you lookin at me so shook.
You know stores don't carry phone
books.

The internet replaced em
made em more worthless than a grain of
soot.
Now they're used as foot rest
to put under the dog's foot.

Me: Listen sir, I don't even want the
whole book.
All I want do is take a quick look.

Store Owner: If that's the case then here give me his
name.

Me: It's my brother and his name is Gee
Brooks.

Store Owner: Gee Brooks?

Me: Yes sir Gee Brooks.

Store Owner: Well Gee Brooks is a famous
skateboarder that
lives in East Brook.

Me: Ok so how do I get there?

Store Owner: Take a right on Ocean St.
Stay on till you get to Sinclaire.
Then make a left on East Brook.
Its right across from the state fair.

My Narration: Then I say to myself I don't need a
road cause my car goes in the air.
So I run back to the car.
Get in and start flying with the wind in
my hair.

Then I land in East Brook waiting on my
brother with a story to share.

I walk up to his front step
knock on his front door.

My Brother: Who is it?

Me: I'm a voice that you can't ignore.

My Brother: brother is that you?

Me: Yes its me now please open the door.

My Narration: I take a look at him and
he's taller than before
clean shave, and he's paid
cause he's definitely not poor.
I look around the place while he takes
me for a tour.
Then he asked why do you look younger
than me and I'm 34?

Me: Well I time traveled here from a year
before.

My Brother: Yeah right what did you really
come here for?

Me: I came here to tell you
about a dream that was an eye sore.

You speed around town
in a car lovers galore.
It was golden an expensive.
I'm sure it was yours.

My Brother: Is that it?

Me: No way B there's a lot more.
You speed across some train tracks
and you hear an engine's roar.
A train hits your car
like a tsunami hits the shore.
You try to get away but you
get crushed by your own door.

My Brother: What was I wearing.

Me: You got killed by a train.
Forget about what you wore.

My Brother: Well I gotta go to the store.

Me: The store?

My Brother: Yea that's right the store.

Me: You got chandeliers on the ceiling.
Marble on the floor.
Why risk your life
going to some dumb store?

Get real my brother.
Open up your core.

My Brother: What's the point of living
if there ain't nothin to live for?
I have money that's whole
but my heart is still tore.

Me: If your heart is what's hurting then
you need to see Jesus Christ Our Lord.

My Brother: I go to church every Sunday and
Wednesday night.
So I already got Jesus in my life

Me: If what you say is true then
you would stay here tonight.
You wouldn't leave earth until you
finished life's fight.
You wouldn't gamble with death
like you do a pair of dice
cause you would be
too busy keepin the faith and shining the light.
You would get on your knees and pray
with all your might.
You would live by faith and not by sight.
You would crack open a Bible.
When the devil tries to bite
you would always try to do what's good
and what's right.
You wouldn't just let your life
blow away like a kite.
And you would do all of the things I said
if you and Jesus was really tight.

My Brother: I can't say I've done those things.
If I did I'd be a lie.
Now you've proven to me that
I don't know Jesus anymore than

the next guy.
Now that I know that I'm hurt
don't want to go to church
still have nothing to live for so
I'm ready to die.

Me: But if you live for Jesus name
you won't live life in vain.
You'll have enough endurance
to endure the pain in Jesus name
cause when you get saved in Jesus name
you won't be the same
cause you'll experience a change.
In Jesus name
people walk that used to be lame
and every time you hear that name
your hairs stand up straight up
like a horse's mane.

In Jesus name life will be
more than just a game
more than the fortune
more than the fame.
Cause in Jesus name
you live your life for eternal gain.

In Jesus name your spirit is free but your
evil desires are restrained.

In Jesus name
your love of drunkenness is tamed
and you won't need to buy a drank
like ya boy T-pain.

In Jesus name
I'm not ashamed, ask me
again I'll tell you just as plain.

But you gone be all right once
you get ordained, in Jesus name.

Cause when you except The Cross
with the blood stains
in Jesus name
Jesus writes your name
in the book of names
and you spend eternity
with your God in your Savior's Name.

You can live life with
Christ starting tonight
if you live it in Jesus name.

My Brother: Why are you preaching to me?
I'm a grown man.

Me: Because I love you and I
want you to understand.

My Brother: Understand? What's to understand?
I can do whatever I want.
I'm American.
And besides I can make my own
decisions
without Jesus to hold my hand.

My Narration: Before I could say another word
my younger brother ran.
He said you can't stop me.
Nobody can.

So I ran out the door
to try to catch the man.
But by time I get outside
he's in the car that's tan.
It shined like gold when
the moonlight expanded.

I get in my car
and by then I'm too late.
The car begins to

accelerate 10 times faster
than a minivan.
By time I catch my breath
he left and all I can say is man!

Me: Lord help me, my brother is gone.
I come to you because I can't catch him
on my own.
Yea I have my Crown Vic, but I can't
even call him on his phone.
Lord if my brother dies, I'd be
like an afro with no comb.

God: Hold on.

Calm your spirit, lower your tone.
You did what you could so, for
the rest, he's on his own.
You have to let him go
so my power can be made known.

You worry about his gold car
with the wheels in chrome.
But I can save your brother
with an ice cream cone.

He will confess my name
when my love is shown.
He will calculate that I saved him
when it registers in his dome.
And when he repents of his
sins, he will know my grace is a free
loan.

Welcome your brother back
like Caesar in ancient Rome
cause after your brother gets
saved. he's coming back home.

My Narration:

After hearing that word from the Lord I
just
lie and wait.
By time I wake up it's
a quarter past 8.
The sun is out, which marks
a new calendar date.
I still worry when I
begin to contemplate
my brother's fate
in which I tried to perpetuate
but really accelerates
the danger I tried to
negate.
So I pray
to God, and He says that
He will alleviate
the trouble I tried to terminate.
The door knob starts to turn, and
I start to hesitate.
The thought that a robber was
coming in, speed up my heart rate.
But when the door opens
I no longer anticipate
it's a robber, because I can appreciate.
The person coming in, cause it was
my younger brother coming in late.

Seeing him walk through door was
like eating a Big Mac.
It was a great experience but it
almost gave me a heart attack.
So then he tells me about his journey
and how he got back.

My Brother's Narration:

When I left to go to the
store I was going to fade to black.
If my life was an album I was
on my last track.
I was flooring it in my
car taking it to the max.
I ignored your words, I didn't face
the facts.
I drove around the city
with the top laid back.
I found myself in another day
when the sunrise cracked.
I traveled so
far I felt like a little rat.

I was running from a feline called
life, cause I was afraid to face my cat.
So like the rat I ran except I was in a
car so I sat.
But what happened next
at the railroad tracks, was crazier than
lighting a candle with a giant
smoke stack.

A bunch of people were crossing the
street
to go to church when I rolled on the
scene.
So I stopped to let them pass, until
the light turned green.
Then I see the
train track you told me about in your
dream.
The gate let down, and the traffic light
shot an emerald beam.

I smoked my tires like sausage.
You could have called me Jimmy Dean.

I went straight for the track when
the train whistle screamed.
I figure by time I got there
I'd be going about 115.

Then smack. I take out the me
myself and I team.
If you know what I mean
I was going to let the train
tear me apart like some old blue jeans.

My legs torn of my car
ripped apart by the seams.
But then before I could do it
and let my life float down the stream.

SLAAMM!

I T-Boned a truck that
sold ice cream. I was ok but my
car was squished as a tangerine.
Then I knew it had to be God
because of how the sunlight gleamed.
But I didn't understand at the time.
That's why I acted all mean.
He offered me a cone.
Then my ears started to steam.
I grabbed his cone and threw down
his ice cream.
He says, "how are you doing sir? Are
you ok?"
I said my car cost more than your house.
You're going to pay.

Ice Cream Man: Hey sir I was supposed to be off today
but my boss said I have to sell ice cream
on Sunday.

My Brother: But nobody buys ice cream unless
it's after May.

Ice Cream Man: I know, but boss said to try it anyway.

My Brother's Narration: Then I said what's the point and what
are you trying to say.

Ice Cream Man: This is an odd coincidence that we would
meet today.

My Brother: Meet?
What do you mean meet?
You wasted my car like an ash tray.
You busted up my car so bad
the CD player won't play.
My top won't let up now it has to stay.
You dented my hood and made the paint
come off now it's gray.
My trunk is in the front.
That's where my cell phone used to lay.

Now it gets no service because you took
it away.
And you talk about some odd
coincidence
we would meet today.
You made things bad enough now get
out of my way.

Ice Cream Man: You know what, you just don't
get it, do you bro?
You think you real smart,
but you really don't even know.
You complain cause ya car got busted up
and the paint won't glow.
You were so worried about yourself you
didn't take the time to catch my flow.
At least you don't have to worry about
makin ya dough.
Once I lose this job, and my boss fire's
me from the ice cream show,

I can't support my family
and my new house goes.
My new clothes
my wife and her new pedicured toes
all that's toast.
Without my job I can't even
take my pants to a tailor to get it sewed
because I'd have to take out a loan
and my creditors would say no.

Zero dollar income, yea that's an all time
low.
But you're over there depressed like
Edgar Allen Poe. But I tell you
make a stand like the Alamo.
Your problems ain't so bad when
you take a walk in my row.
After you go home you should feel
like Tickle Me Elmo
when you look at your life.

Compared to mine when you catch my
flow.

My Brother: Tickle Me Elmo you must be kidding.
Just because I'm rich doesn't mean
Everything is Jell-O pudding.
I've accomplished so much
life ain't worth living.

Yea I got money like the opera
but my heart is not singing.
It's just sitting
Waiting
to get hit by a train that's
moving.

I really don't care about the car, it's
just my soul that needs soothing.

Ice Cream Man: But that's why you've been blessed.
You better be glad you were in
that car wreck.
That car would have been
mangled by that giant train set.

Your neck
your whole chest
would have been destroyed
when you and the train met.

You would have breathed
your last breath
the years you could have had would have
been any man's guess.

Your grave would have said rest in peace
but you would have been in pieces when
you rest.
But the man that you thought was
a pest
protected you from your own death
like a bullet proof vest.

And God gave you a second chance
to do what He request.
Trouble comes to us just to test
whether we should stay or fly away from
the earth nest.

But in your case he choose to let
mercy guide your last few steps
cause if it wasn't for mercy you'd be
a mess, you'd be dead from the tread
that the big train sets. Sure I may
be in debt for getting the company truck
in a slam fest.
But God was able to save your life with
some ice cream

cones and a car wreck. And because of
that
you and I are still blessed.

My Brother:

You know what, man this thing is finally
making sense.
You and my brother tried to tell me the
truth and I was too dense
to be wise and realize what it really
meant.
I was about to kill myself, but like an
angel
you were sent.
To save my life at the ice cream truck's
dispense.

Who cares about my car dent
or the hood that's bent.
They'd get sucked up in a big vacuum
as if a tornado went.
Because they're about as valuable as
to me a piece of carpet lent.
My brother saw it in a dream
and he gave me a big hint.
But I didn't listen cause I thought my life
was
spent
like sucked out candy faded out stripes
on a peppermint.
I thought I was old news so I put my
heart
out for rent.

Then I realized that Jesus bought
my soul under the agreement
that He would die on a cross just
so man and God can live like God meant
and now all I have to do is repent.

My Brother's Narration: So knowing that, me and the ice
cream man walk
across the cement.
To get to the other
side of the street pavement.

Then I can go to the church I saw earlier,
to get some appeasement.
There I get baptized, with water to be
rinsed.
After that I go back to my mansion,
that for humility sake I'll call a sleep
tent.

And that's what happened from the time
I left my street fence to the time I came
back
and told my story's chain of events.

Me: So you finally learned what Jesus is all
about.
You learned God saved you without a
doubt.
You know I prayed when you left the
house.
I thought you were adding another life to
the
death toll count.

But when you bounced God answered
the
word of prayer that I pronounced.
And He said He could save you with an
ice cream
cone that's what he announced. And I
was shocked, reluctant to believe the
1st ounce.
But God in his mysterious ways is
something

you can't denounce.
Comparing his ways to mine like
comparing a microbiologist to the
microscopic louse.

The difference in the knowledge is
an indescribable amount.
So when I heard the word of God to wait
it out
on the couch
then I had to stay here and not pout.
Even though I wanted to go south
and search around the city to
find your whereabouts.

But I couldn't, cause God said to lay low
like a mouse.
It was hard, but when you came back
I was ready to shout.
He saved you after all, inside and out.
He let me watch your life, and how you
grew from
short and stout, to long and tall.
Like a water spout.

I watched you play in ya crib
when you were just a sprout.
The only way you could get out
is to tug on your mother's blouse.
Nowadays the only way we can even
see eye to eye is if you crouch.
You got saved and all you need
is Christ without a doubt.

You won't be sad for long
if clean up your act, and put good words
in ya mouth.

Remember when you're in pain God is
always there to heal the ouch.
So on that note I must go and continue
my journey abroad and throughout.

My Brother: Wait don't go, you just got here a little while ago.

Me: I know I should leave bread crumbs so I
never forget The route. I'll swim back
through here like the rainbow trout.
But for now I gotta be like the GI Joe
and the string under his pouch.
When you pull it the door closes
and I'm over and out.

PART III

My Narration:

Easy-peasy-lemon-squeezey.
Now that my brother's saved
everything's
all breezy.
I can do whatever I want cause my car
is off the heazy.

I can blow up the Eiffel Tower just
because
it pleases me.
Then I use my car to rewind it back
before
anybody sees me.
I can tear up your lab like Dexter's sister
named Dee Dee.
Then I can go back in time and put it
back
neatly.
If I wanted to fight nobody could beat
me
cause I could skip through time so you
couldn't
defeat me.

I'm invincible, on top of the world I'm
the
television part of the TV.
Besides I could blast you back in time
to the BC.
Give you to the T-Rex when he
roars feed me.
Then I could press the fast forward
button and skip over ya like a track
on the CD.

Then tell you what's going to happen
like the news paper that comes out
weekly.
I could buy an antique pen that was
made cheaply.
Then I could come back to the future and
sell it for 3Gs.

You know what I think I'll go back
in time and get a tee pee.
Then sell it to a museum so they
can treat me.
And make me so rich bill Gates
will want to be me.

So I set the time machine for
1500 and I drive to the land of the
Cherokee.
I was afraid to trade with the Comanche
and the Apache, I needed to find a tribe
that was a little more
friendly.
Plus in the year 1500 is before the British
colonies.

I try to slow the car and I crash land into
a tree.
But luckily
everything still works like the ignition
and the key.
So I hide the car up in the bushes
so the people won't see.

I walk around the woods and all I see is
me.
No food, no water, no signs of a tee pee
until I squint my eyes and see something
smoky.
People gatherin around a fire

the whole t-r-o-p.
Some look to be dancing
like Hokey Pokey.
I better go over there quietly
before they take those razor sharp arrows
and poke me.

So I slowly make my way up the hill
that I was scooping.
I wanted to cover up my scent so
I rubbed my clothes with an oak leaf.
Try to sneak up to their fire so I
can look more closely.
But they just look at me and wave like
they
know me.
Take me to our leader I said
in a voice that spoke deep.

Me: Where ya peoples at?
Where ya folks be?

Tribal Man: What is it that you want with
the Chief Cahochee?

Me: Is he your leader?

Tribal Man: Yes.

Me: So then where is Cabone Tree?

Tribal Man: It is Cahochee.

Me: Whatever.

Tribal Man: No whatever you don't disrespect our
own Chief.

Me: I'm sorry sir.

Tribal Man: You are forgiven.

Me: So now can I see Chief Cahochee?

Tribal Man: Yes but don't come at him too fast
approach him like you approach
me.
Just don't yell this time and
walk very slowly.
He's very old and sick he's probably
in his hut soaking.

My Narration: So I tip toe to the hut of Chief
Cahochee.
I walk in and he's surrounded
by chickens and other live poultry.
Come in, come in he says.
I am the great Chief Cahochee.

Me: Cahochee, yeah you sound like a
real OG.

Cahochee: What's OG?

Me: Oh just some term I learned in the
future
After 04 or 03.

Me: So Mr. Cahochee, OG, or 03
whatever
you want to be.

Cahochee: It's Cahochee.

Me: Right Mr. Cahochee.

Me: I was just wandering if I could
borrow say a whole tee pee?

Cahochee: What, are you trying to hoax me?

Me: Calm down, calm down, this is not a joke
Bee.

Cahochee: A whole tee pee?

Me: If I stuttered or choked
then excuse me.

But I don't think I did so yes I want
the whole tee pee.

Cahochee: For what so you can peek out of it and
scope me.

Me: No, I just want to make it a museum
show piece.

Cahochee: No, you cannot take a whole tee pee.
Red Foot, Little Bear toss this man out of
here give him a good throw, please.

Me: Wait a minute let me go, why you gotta
scapegoat me?

Cahochee: Because you smell like trouble and dead
oak leaves.

Me: Well, at least I don't smell like molded
cheese
or green paint marks on my body lookin
like frozen peas.

Tribal Man: How dare you mock our tribal marks?
Rope him to the top of the oak trees
then drop him to the ground on his legs
so he can walk with broken knees.

Me:	Ok, you know what, why don't I just take the rope and leave.
Tribal Man:	Hmmm, what do you think Chief Cahochee?
Cahochee:	Let him take the rope, but make sure he leaves.
My Narration:	So they give me the rope and I start to believe even though they won't give me the tee pee I can use this rope to something so there's still hope for me. So tied the rope to my car and tied the other end to the tee pee. Then I went back to the year 2033. The year of my brother of course and shoes with CDs. I switch to 8th gear with the tee pee and blast out of the land of the Cherokee. I speed down the Boulevard with the tee pee behind me. It caught people off guard. Beep, beep I give people a warning so my car doesn't run anybody over like the butt of a cigar cause, my tee pee may be soft but my bumper is still hard. I gotta get this thing to museum before I see the nighttime star

cause they close at sunset and that
doesn't seem to be too far.

At this point, if I'm late I'll seem like a
house with
no yard.
A butter farmer with no lard
cause anyone who has a tee pee for no
reason looks just as dumb as a
Christmas tree on a father's day card.

Then I arrive at the museum just as I
figure
out how much they charge.

Ticket Man: $50 please.

Me: What you must be kidding me I'm just here to
in barge.
I mean barge in, you know what I mean.
I don't want to pay a sum that large.

Ticket Man: Where's your name on the guest list, what
movies have you stared.

Me: None.

Ticket Man: Ok then $50 is the charge.

Me: Here take it, but at least I didn't get a
haircut
by a clippe, some clippers with no "r".
Bald on one side afro on the other.
So I think I'll call you Homer Simpson
Marge.
I'd call your manager, but with that half
military
haircut I'll ask for your lieutenant sarge.

Ticket Man: This haircut is the style nowadays.

So get off my case par.

Me: Take it easy man I just want to see who's in charge.

Ticket Man: If that's all you wanted why didn't just call Mr. Shimar.
Besides you can't joke on my haircut if you got
a tee pee behind your car.

My Narration: Then I take off running as I wave goodbye to
the crazy haircut clerk guy.

I look around for the manager named Shimar.
Then I bump into a man with a dark blue tie
"Can I help you" he says with a pestered look in his eye.

Me: Yes I need to see the manager they call Shimar.

My Narration: "Right here" he says with an exasperated sigh.

Me: What's wrong I said, you look like voter that's
been disenfranchised.

Shimar: "Voting's, the last of my problems when I look up
at the sky.
I feel like a 747 jumbo jet that won't fly."

Me: Why?

Shimar: Because I own the biggest museum in town
and people look at my tickets and don't buy.
My museum doesn't intrigue people like suspense movies, or motion picture sifi.
It's like they're rainforest wet
and I'm desert dry.
Nobody comes in here, not even to say hi.

Me: Well I have the solution
to your problem, to you dry.
You need to get more authentic.
You're like a pastry shop with no pie.
You may have the biggest store but you have no supplies.
If your museum were a baby it wouldn't even
have tears when it cried.
So to solve your problem you need to put moisture
in the baby's eye.
Then the mother can help the baby
with the maternal instincts that she may apply.

Shimar: "What are you trying to say?" "Kiss this museum goodbye?"

Me: No all I'm saying is that you need something alive.

Shimar: "Huh."

Me: Why use a picture when you can have the real guy?
I can use a time machine slash car Crown Vic thing
that can fly.

You might have Chinese food on display but I can
uncover the man who invented stir fry.
You cross every "T" dot every "I", but I can find the men
who invented the English language
before the first man said hi.

Shimar "Show me the time machine I want to buy."

Me: This time machine is not for sale but I'll let you
have what the time machine is roped to and tied
I have a big original Cherokee tee pee and I'll
sell it to you for 3,005.

Shimar: "Done deal, for 3,005."

Me: Here's the tee pee, but your authentic sword collection is a lie.
I'm going back to the land of shoguns to get you
a real samurai
and when come back I want 5.

Shimar: "5 what?"

Me: I want my pay to be 5,005.

My Narration: So I can go back in time and make money
without having to try.
So in a flash it's back to the land where the samurais are.
16th century Japan where armors still in tact.

Hey Mr. Japanese man with the funny looking hat.
Where are the samurais that
rule the land and have the heavy padding on the back?

Kamoripat: You're looking at one named Kamoripat.

Me: The only person I see is you, and you're not Kamoripat.
You're wearing a big dress and you're too fat.
The only thing you're a warrior of is a 2 pack of
hot dogs and a Big Mac.

Kamoripat: **RRRR AAhhhh!**
I am Kamoripat.

My Narration: Then he rips his clothes off and reveals his armor that's stacked.
He was so mad he took out his sword and started to take a whack.
I ran away from the sword before he
cut the curtain to my life act.

DING! he hit the sword on the ground and made the rock crack.

Kamoripat: I'll get you, you little rat.

My Narration: I take off running before he screams that.

Me: Catch me if you can, you might want to use the recap.
That armor makes you slow keeping you from bending your

knee cap.
So the only way to catch me is by getting your speed back.
Doesn't look like that's happening so hit the rewind
button or like I said use that recap.
Until then I'll see you later Kamoripat, cause I gotta scat.

Kamoripat: "When I catch you I'll slice
you up and make you my doormat."

My Narration: After he said that I took off like the Amtrak
ran into the woods like a book goes into a knapsack.

Once I go in it seemed like all the light just retract.
I'm in the woods and every things pitch black.
But I keep running pushing my body
to the max.
Then I run out of the woods and see a bunch of
roofs stacked.
Then I run closer to see that
the roof stacks
are really a bunch of Japanese houses within one
village pack.

So run in one of the Japanese houses to relax.
I'm so tired I don't think forward I think back.
If I don't lay down, I'll get arrest cardiac.
So I find a bed, plop down and lay flat.

Then I get under the covers and let my blanket wrap.

Man of the House: What are you doing in my house?

Me: I was tired so I'm taking a nap.

Man of the House: Well why are you so tired?

Me: I was running from Kamoripat.

Man of the House Kamoripat?

Me: Yes isn't that what I said do I have to repeat that?

Man of the House Why are you running from Kamoripat?

Me: Because I said he wasn't a samurai and that he
looked really fat. Now he wants to cut me up
and make me his doormat.

Man of the House: So you insulted his honor.

Me: No I just said the only thing he's warrior of is a 2 pack of hot dogs and a Big Mac.

Man of the House: What else did you do?

Me: On nothing I just may have insulted his hat.

Man of the House: So you did insult his honor, you little sap.

Me: So what if I did, he can get over it, I shake his hand and give him some dap.

Man of the House: No, you fool he has to get you back.

Me:	By calling me names?
Man of the House:	No, by killing you in a sword fight match.
Me:	Alright, ok, I'm going to hide under that rack.
Man of the House:	No.
Me:	Why not Jack?
Man of the House	1st of all my name is not Jack.
Me:	You didn't give me your name, so I had to pull one of the stack.
Man of the House:	My name is Zackarijji but you can just call me Zack.
Me:	Cool so I'm going to hind under that rack. Zack: No No No. You will not put me or my family in danger of attack.
Me:	So protect me like offensive lineman does the quarterback. Besides he doesn't want to harm you he just wants to pay me back.
Zack:	Ok fine but you owe me big time.
Me:	Ok Mr. Zack.
Zack:	Kamo-Kamo-Kamo-Kamoripat.

Me: Where is the big lumix?

Kamoripat: I hear that.
I know you're in this house I can hear your feet tap.

Me: Wow, you've stated the obvious you deserve a big clap.

Kamoripat: **Yaahhh!**, when I find you I'll cut your
tongue off so you won't chat.
Then I'll cut you up and make you a doormat.

My Narration: While he's yelling I'm setting up a trap.

Me: Hey Kamoripat how do you keep on that funny looking helmet without a chin strap?

Kamoripat: **Aahhh** where are you, you little brat.

Me: Right here under the tall rack.

My Narration: Then he runs over to where I am so he can attack.
But then he trips over the string between the walls
that I attached.
Then he hits his head on the rack and falls
flat on his back. He's still alive but he'sout cold like an ice pack.
"Big help you were," I say to Zack.

Zack:	Well, at least I let you use my house as a safe shack.
My Narration:	"Yeah whatever" I say as I pick up Kamoripat. I carry him to my car and throw him in the back. Then I return to Mr. Shimar's museum with a samurai still in tact. And then he repays me with a 5,005 dollar stack.
Me:	Hey Mr. Shimar you know what would bring you more guests? A pirate exhibit with a real pirate chest. In fact I bet it will make you more money in one day than the samurai's life time best.
Shimar:	Ok well how much do you want?
Me:	1.5 million, the profit will take care of the rest. If you don't believe me then we can put it to the test.
Shimar:	Ok but you better hold up your end of the desk because if you don't you'll have my whole business in debt.
Me:	Don't worry Shimar I'll have your pirate exhibit before you can breathe your next breath.
My Narration:	So I get in my car to get to a place

with a pirate chest.
Year 1300, pirates ain't got there yet.
So I flip the switch a few hundred years
past the previous one set.

Then I flip the wheels and turn on the
jets.
Finally I see a pirate ship flag topped off
with the crows nest.
I crash onto the ship and say I'm
here to collect my treasure chest.

Pirate: Ha, Ha, Ha, Ha, Ha, Ha.

My Narration: The head pirate laughs with his parrot
pet.

Pirate: You ain't collecting nothing here except
the emptiness
that you had in your hand before you left.
For, I am Black Beard, now get off me
ship before we put ye to death.

Me: Black Beard, man, it would be a real
honor to take your chest.

Black Beard: That's it boy you're walking the plank.

My Narration: Oh no, I'm in a mess.
Black Beard pokes me with a sword
every time
I take a step.
Now I'm one stride away from drowning
in the ocean's depth.

Me: Before you throw me overboard like
<u>Pirates of theCaribbean</u> Johnny Depp.

Can I say some last words before I die
in a sea as vast as the internet?

Black Beard and Pirates: Go ahead matee all in favor say yep.

"Yep, yep, yep" the crew agrees.
So say your last words with some pep.

Me: What did you say?

Black Beard: Hurry up or we'll kick you off the plank.
That's a promise not a threat.

Me: Ok then I just wanted to say when I
crashed into the ship deck
I made a hole in the ship and if you
don't get off you'll get shipwrecked.

Black Beard: Arrgg, let's go crew, we have to get
in the row boats before water makes the
ship offset.

Me: What about me?

Black Beard: Ha, ha, you stay and cook in the sun
like a fired egg.
Then cool off while your drowning body
floats
To the water's edge.

My Narration: They take off and I laugh because my car
can fly like Jango Fett.

I grab all the merchandise I can find.
Then I take the treasure chest.

Then I blast back to the future year
with my time traveling gear.
Then I show Shimar the treasure chest

that he spent so much money on to invest
and he's amazed so he writes me a
check,
1.5 million.
Now I'm a millionaire overnight who
would have guessed.

Me: Hey Shimar.

Shimar: Yes my money making time traveler that
I adore.

Me: Enough with the small talk I need a
refrigidiginiga.

Shimar: You mean a refrigidiginator?

Me: Yeah whatever, the thing that instantly
freezes
meat so it's easier to store.

Shimar: Yes I have one what do you need it for.

Me: So I can freeze people instantly and put
them
on the floor.
They won't be dead, they'll just be stiff
as a board.
Plus it's a lot quicker than tricking
savage
samurais into hitting their head on a rack
near a door.

Shimar: Ok then here's a refrigidiginator.
Go get King Arthur's sword.

My Narration: So I go back in time, freeze King Arthur
and take his sword stuck in the rock
like a socket out of a power cord.

Then I jump back to Shimar's time
and give Shimar the sword
where he dumps in my hand another cash reward.

Then I go back in time to the Norwegian shore. I trick the Vikings there by telling them
I'm the Thunder god Thor.
Then I froze them with the refrigidiginator.
The ice is only temporary, they'll just wake up sore
after that I grab the helmets and take the hats
that they wore.
Back to the museum, another cash reward.

Me: You know what Mr. Shimar you need a dinosaur.

My Narration: So I freeze 3 Velociraptors.
Take em back to Shimar's store.
Ching ching another cash reward.

Me: You know what I want to see Julius Caesar
before he was assassinated by the senators.

My Narration: I get in the car, freeze him up and put him by the door.

DUMP! in my hands lands

another cash
reward.

Then I go back to ancient Greece to get the Trojan horse.

BAM! another cash reward.

I go back in time to get rare artifacts from the
year 1004.

SLAM! Another cash reward.

I go back in time to freeze general from the
Civil War.

SHAZAM! another cash reward.

I go back in time to get Shaka Zulu and his clothes he tore.

WHAM! another cash reward.

I go back in time freeze King Ramsey in his slumber snore.

POOF! the dust settles and no cash reward.

Me: What do you mean no cash reward?

Shimar: I gave you so much money you make King Midas
look poor.

Me: So who cares, I just want more.

Shimar: I gave you 30 million dollars, I'm broke.
Man I just can't afford.

Me: Forget you then Shimar I'm walking out the door.
It's about time I bought myself something nice. I got 30 million to show for.
This Crown Victorian is kind of old I might need to restore.

My Narration: So go to a car dealership, buy a real expensive fast getaway car called the GT made by Ford.

I got it with the white and blue stripes.
So if someone sees it they won't ignore.
Driving this car I'll never get bored.
Then I hire a car mechanic to get the time traveling stuff out the Victorian and back to the GT Ford.
Then I tipped him a million dollars to show him there wasn't anything I can't pay for.
Then I ship the old Crown Victorian to a big theme park roller coaster lovers galore.

Ching ching they pay me a 10 million dollar cash reward.
Then I drive around town with my new Ford.
Hit the accelerator, 0-60 in 3.4.
Bob and weave through traffic going faster and faster as my engine roar

My Narration: YAAAAAHHHHOOOO!

my car is going almost 204.

SLAM!

I hit a car with a woman and
little girl. And I hit the side with
the little
girl's door.
It was almost like the dream that
my brother's car got tore.
Except I caused this one to happen
and it's more real than before.

PART IV

Me: Man, look at what I've done.

My Narration: I get out the car to see the mother and she's stunned.

Me: Ma'am I'm so sorry.

The Mother: Tell it to my youngest one
and maybe to my oldest son.
While you out joy riding having your fun
you almost killed my daughter on your
little test run.

My daughter was a beautiful girl didn't
even suck
on her thumb.
My daughter was smart, you'd ask her a
math question.
She always knew the sum.

My daughter had heart, even though 11th
year
on earth hadn't begun.
And you, you don't even care about my
little hun.

I guess you're just the big cheese, and
my 10 year
old daughter's just a crumb.
I bet we're just getting in your way
because
you beat to your own drum.

You probably think we don't matter to
you. We're
just a bunch of hoodlums.

Well I got news for you, you
rich arrogant piece of scum.
You can't just go 200 mph and step on
everyone else like piece of gum.

My Narration: I go to the car to try to time travel
and undo what I had just done.
Then the woman in the car pulls
out a gun.

The Mother: "Get out of the car, what do you think I'm
dumb?
You think I'm just gonna let you drive
away to your
spot in the sun?
Oh, no you're taking my daughter to the
hospital on Boulevard and Junction."

Me: But, but, but.

The Mother: "Shut up.
You caused this accident, you've said
enough."

My Narration: So we get in and drive past the Pizza Hut
as she holds her daughter in her arms like
a cup.
I rush down the Boulevard to find where
Junction
begins.
And I find take the turn as I see the road
bends.
I roll down Junction until I see an
ambulance drive in.

The Mom: "There it is right there with the
roof made of tin."

My Narration: After that we run inside to try to wait in
the den.

But the mother didn't want to stop then.
"Take me to an operating room now,"
she said
Then a nurse says "Ok ma'am floor 10."

So as the mother runs up to the elevator
carrying her daughter like a mother hen
she runs into a surgeon named Ben.

The Mother: Listen, I need help, my daughter
needs an operation before her life ends.

Dr. Ben: Ok but I might have to operate under the skin.

The Mother: Just do it, so my daughter can wake up
and I can
see her precious grin.

My Narration: After she says that they take her to the room
where they do all the operating in.

The Mother: You can go now I just wanted you to drop off my child.
Go out and continue your reckless selfish lifestyle.

Me: No I'm staying here I'm not really that wild.
I just got carried away I'm usually calm and mild.
I usually straight as a ruler square as a floor tile.

The Mother: Well I'm sorry I pulled that gun on you,

I'm not
one to kill people, I'm not really that vile.
It's just that I'd give anything to see her smile.
She's all I have left of my husband Kyle.

Me: What do you mean?

The Mother: He died in a fire along with my oldest son Miles.
The only remnant of a family I have is 2 obituaries
in an old file
and my little daughter's smile.
If I lost her I'd cry a river longer than the Nile.

My Narration: I grab the intercom and the front desk is what
I dial.

Me: Get me a chair I say, so this woman can sit down for a while.

My Narration: Then I see a nurse walk up with and put a chair in the aisle.

The Mother: Thank you for the chair, and listening to the pain that I know.
I shouldn't have got my pistol out like some kind of psycho.

Me: Don't worry ma'am, I know you've been through
some tough trials.

My Narration: We waited in the hall until the hour hand went around

3 cycles.
The doctor came out like the batteries got pulled out of his RC Tyco.

Me: What's wrong doc you look like a turned out light bulb.

Dr. Ben: It's your daughter.

Mother: Is it her I-phone?
Is it my Geico?
Is it her new nice coat?
If so then it can all go, I'm just concerned with
her life's hope.

Dr. Ben: It's not about the coat, it's not about your Geico.

Mother: Then what is it about, did your surgical tool get her eye poked?

Dr. Ben: No it's not about her eye scope.

Mother: What is it about?

Dr. Ben: Your daughter's life hope.

Mother: And.

Dr. Ben: She didn't make it despite yours and my hope.

Mother: # NO,NO,NO!!!

My Narration: The mother breaks down into tears
in my arms to fold.
And I embrace her and my arms do hold.

I sit her down and rub her back as the
tears from the cry roll.
And I feel the pain she's going through
except in a 3 fold, tri-fold
because I'm responsible for the death.

I feel 3 times as cold
and 1/3rd as bold.
All I can do is watch a mother's outpour
for her 11 year old.

The Mother:

The child that fit so perfectly in my
parental mold.
The child that was worth more to me
than gold.
The child that if I was
offered diamonds for her I wouldn't have
sold.
The child that I birthed and rocked her
to sleep with the lullabies I told.
The child that meant so much to me she
made my
balled up heart unfold.
The child that lit my candle of joy and
made it explode.
The child that took this world so cold
and put it into her heart to hold.
Now that child that occupied
so much of my soul
was taken away, and all that's left is
a big empty hole.

My Narration:

After she said that I felt real low
on the totem pole.
I took away that woman's gift and left
her
a piece of coal.
The only thing that will keep me from
crying is a sermon from Osteen, Joel.

Front Desk:	Ma'am, you need to come back and fill out our death toll.
Mother:	Why do I have to fill out a death toll? Because we have to report all of the dead patients that were enrolled.
Mother:	"Alright I'll fill it out but you better help me."
My Narration:	She says crying as she scolds.
Mother:	I just lost my daughter so I'm heading down a tough road.
My Narration:	After she uttered that sentence I bit the dust and hit the road. I couldn't hang around for this episode. Because I'm the leading antagonist. I play the bad guy role. Big buffoon that takes out, lays out a little girl with the car that he rode.

The guilt is eating me up inside.
If I see the mother's face again I think
I'll implode.
The deepest anxiety of my heart will
come out of my nose.
When I see that woman's face the guilt
makes my spirit corrode.
Pretending everything's ok when it's not,
I can no longer impose.

So I run out to my car so I can fix the
trouble that arose.

I get in an try to set the time traveling mode.
I see the time forward switch, but I can't find a reverse for things of the past onward.

Me: **Oh No! NNNOOO!**

To the past I can't go
unless I take it back to the mechanic.
Yeah maybe he would know
how to fix a time machine with the past remote.
Then he could fix my bumper that looks like
it's been tore up by a Billy goat.

My Narration: So I get in the Ford GT and that's all she wrote.

Zoom I just drove onto Fine Oats.
The street that holds the location of the dealership and the line ropes
that guard the sought after mechanic in his ivory tower castle moat.

But his drawbridge opens up to those who
have a big money boat.
So I can pay him about 2 mill to
get my time machine afloat
and my bumper that slammed into the car and got broke.

So I walk to the famous mechanic
like Arnold Schwarzenegger

Me: How long will it take?

Mechanic: 2 or 3 hours I don't know.

My Narration: "I'll be back" I say as I give him the 2
keys
with 2 nuggets of gold
that I give him for the 2 million I owed.
Time machines are expensive especially
ones that
have the tires that fold.

So I jog around the block and come back
and the mechanic tells me everything's
fixed sir you can go.

Me: What about the time machine and the
past mode?

Mechanic: Well I would have to build a reverse flex time
sipper, but
I don't have one of those.
I'm sorry sir all I could do is put a new
sound system
in a brand new Bose.

Me: Forget the Bose

My Narration: and get the car and bust through the glass
with poles.
I try to be a hero
and cut the grass blades of wrong doing
and I can't even mow.

I'm not mad at my role I'm not mad at
the show.
I'm mad at the writer and to him my
anger flows.

Why did you let this happen God? Why

didn't you let me go? Why did you
take my good intentions and feed it to
the crows?

God Speaks

God:

Who are you to get loud with me?
If you throw a punch do I say ow you hit
me?
Who are you to raise your voice at me?
I can close your eyes and make you blind
as a bat that can't see.
Who are you to contend with the
Almighty?

Can you close my eyes and blind sight
me?
If you get irritated can you open your
mouth and bite me?
Can you even stare at the sun that shines
so brightly?
Put your hands away, you can't fight me.

I made the night sky, and the moon and
the stars to light thee.
What is your life to me
but a vapor that rises at night and gets
carried
away by a breeze.

You can't even take a step unless I bend
your knee.
You couldn't even take in air, until I put
wind in your lungs to breathe.

You can't read, you can't sneeze, you
can't breed.
You can't feed, you can't do anything
without me

or if you disagree
name one thing you can do without me
and I'll tell you how I'm the only one
who instilled
the power within thee.

Take for instance you going to make
your little
money.
You thought it was a little funny
to take my power for granite and run
from me
so you could trade artifacts older than
Egyptian mummies.

You built a false god,
when there's only one me.
I'm the Eternal God, your god was made
of 20s.
You followed your false god into the
passenger's seat
into a car that contained my children's
children's seed.

You think you can rewind time but the
only master of time is me.
1000 years to you is just one day that I
see
because of your foolishness, you made
one of my daughters
rest in peace.

You call yourself the hero but yet your
power rest in me.
You call yourself the all knowing yet you
get
mad at me
because I don't save you from your
foolish deeds.

You're like an ant to me chewing on
clueless meat.
So someone else died because of the
foolishness you eat.

You should thank me, that you sowed
foolishness
and death you did not reap.
I had mercy on you, and left your soul to
keep.
I do not forget about the others—that
morn and weep
worn and weak.

Life is hard on a soul that seeps
down in life's winters cold and bleak.
Everyone has a tough season
they have to meet
but those who stay close to my feet
those are the ones who get the eternal
treat.

You went astray so I gave you a wakeup
beep.
Come back to me,
I know your every heartbeat.
I am strong as the lion,
yet gentle as the sheep.
Those who come back to me I'm always
happy
to greet.

I lift up the humble, and down trotted
give
victory to those in defeat.
Blessed are those who carry everything
to me.
For it is written the Earth shall be
inherited

by the meek.

Remember what I've told you, remember
everything
I've taught.
Stay true to my words, and now I leave
you in peace.

My Narration:

Wow, what can I say after that.
I now realize the error of my ways and
I'm
ready to change back
freezing historical figures all for money
stacks.
Man what kind of mess was that?
That was whack.

But now I'm renewed in my God pact.
But only through Jesus Christ carrying
The Cross
on His back.

I was livin in lies and He was the one
that helped
me face the facts.
That girl's death put a hole in me and
God filled up
the gap.
My guilt attacked
but God came in and ransacked
all the emotions that were inside of me
and made me feel like crap.

I still need to undo what I did so
I can relax.

But without going in the past I don't
know
what kind of solution is attached.

Trial and error trying on each hat until I can find a solution to get that little girl's life back.

Me: Lord let me do this for your glory and give you the decorated plaque

PART V

My Narration: New part of my life new chapter.
No longer am I making money by
freezing raptors.
I gotta do right so I can be in the rapture.
I've been renewed so God's word I can
capture.
I gotta feed souls like the fellow pastor.

Me: Lord if I keep your covenant I too shall
lie in green pastures.
Money and God, a man can only serve
one master.

If I serve God first then if He wills He
will make
my wallet fatter.
But if I live life to serve money my own
soul will end
in disaster.
So I serve God and do what He ask first.
Then I let him take care of my needs,
give me water
when I have thirst.

Lord I know you can make a way out of
no way.
You put the sun up and made a new day.
You're so powerful you can make North
America touch Zimbabwe.

I came to this piece to tell my future self
what to say.
But then problems came up and I got
lead astray
but after I find out how to go back to the
past

when I resolve this conflict, on God is
where my eyes will stay.

At first
I was on Christ every verse.
Then went off and tried to increase my
worth
and I hit the woman's child that she gave
birth.
Because of my carelessness somebody
else got hurt.

"The horror, the horror "I felt like Joseph
Conrad's Mr. Kurts.
When I sat down and got the bad news
from the nurse
I felt like the robber that stole a purse.
The fact that I caused it made me feel
even worse
but it was God that picked me up so I can
go on and do his work.

Now I'm fresh as a daisy washed clean
like a new shirt.
Now that I'm talking about clothes I
need to address the
past before it skirts.
So I can save the future from the past
that I deterred.
So we can move on and not go back to
the old ways
and not revert.

I drive the Ford GT into the sunrise.
Flip the wheels, put on the new jets so I
can fly.
Tilt the nose up to the sky.

Hold onto the steering wheel and raise up high
so I can go fast without the risk of hitting someone elses ride.

I pray Jesus humbles me so I won't have any pride.
Put the thrusters on and I'm going 755.
Man I'm going faster than a Ferrari 575.
Except I'm going an extra 555.

Zoom I see a red blur go by.
Is it Superman, the Flash, Spiderman?
Who is that guy
that blew by me going 755.
I try to follow him, but this man's turbo is
quicker than the eye.

I look around and don't even see the G-U-Y.
I know I'm not drunk, never committed a D-U-I.
But I must be hallucinating, I know a man can't fly
and disappear before my very eyes.

Then I get a knock knock on my window
and I see the guy, that blew by
and he says "I."

Me: I what?

Syron: I am The Syron from Butt Kicking Enterprise.

Me: So you want to mug me?

Syron: No I'm one of the good guys.

Me: Do you need a ride.

Syron: Yeah my thrusters are fried.

Me: Ok then get inside.

My Narration: So the Syron gets in and puts on his seatbelt.
Then he touches around the interior and says
"is that felt?"

Me: No it's leather.

Syron: Oh my bad electronic gloves probably altered what I felt.

Me: So how does that suit work anyway, and, what was that
smell I smelt?

Syron: Ha ha ha ha whoever smelt it be the one that dealt.

Me: I didn't make that smell or a fart that smells like pigeon pelts.

Syron: Ha, ha, ha, ha I think I just gave you a brain welt.
Relax kid that smell is programmed to let me know when my rocket fuel melts.

Instead of having an annoying alarm that yelps
I just got the stench, since I can't see my fuel run out the
smell really helps.
So I have to ride in your car until my combustor completely
refuels itself.

Me: So Syron what do you do for a livin?
If your fuels out, all our shoes are good
for is grillin.

Syron: Yeah, yeah keep the jokes coming you're lucky
I'm just chillin.
But I find my life to be thrillin.
I take a bite out of crime and make the
criminals get tooth fillin.
They call me the Syron because I'm red
and blue like the police car that catches
em stealin.
When I jet over to the criminals
warehouse they're
through dealin.
They try to shoot at me but I just blast
off come
back and give em another feelin.
I dodge all their attacks power up on em
like
<u>Dragon Ball Z</u> Krillen.
Then I beat em just enough to make an
impact so the crime won't look appealin.
Then I let the cops take em to the big
house, the jail cell buildins.
I'm a construction worker, when I'm not
pouring out justice and over spillin.
And if I'm not getting a cat out of a tree
then I'm probably drillin
a hole in the wall so I can put up ya
ceilin.
I used to be a cop so I could stop the
killin,
but now they call me the Syron, fighting
street thug villains.

Me: If you used to be a cop how did you lose
ya badge?

Syron: Let's just say I made the wrong people at the wrong time mad.
I was under cover doing a bust, and they thought I was bad.
I was acting like a pusher so I could find out a tad
more than the other cops so they could get more info than they had.
The cooks find out I'm under cover even though I thought
I had the gift of gab.
I go to visit my father not knowing they were
following the cab.
I go inside and they peel the door open like a scab.
There's 2 of em, one took out a pocket knife ready to stab.
The other one pulled a gun on my dad.
So I pull my gun out and shoot him before he shoots my dad.
He falls on the ground and his partner runs out like I'm a seagull
and he's the beach crab.
The cops show up and they think I'm the one that's bad.
I tell em I'm undercover, and I was just protectin my dad.
Then I go to chief's office and he's so dense like an old submarine
iron clad.

Even though I can't do police work I'm still not sad
cause when I put on the suit and do justice and I'm still glad.

Me: So how did you become the Syron in the 1st place?

Syron: It all happened after I lost my job trying to solve the case.
It was like I was consumed by the police work, it took up all my thought space.
The one day I take off early I lose the only job that keeps
my family's income at a steady pace.
So then I get a construction job so I can bring home the bacon
and put it on the dinner plate.
But the loss of my job, and the guilt stung in my eyes like mace.

Yeah I got another job but I was still missing something.
You could see it in my face.
I was getting fat without any criminals to chase.
Every time I saw a robber get away in the news I felt like a disgrace.

I felt like a human on The Planet of the Apes.
A retired zoo keeper that let gorillas run around in capes.
Yeah sure criminals aren't monkeys, but they shouldn't be in in the streets so they can be on showcase.
Just the thought of unpunished crime gives my tongue a distaste.

I'm still a police officer at heart even though for construction
my badge has been replaced.
I still needed that daily satisfaction of doing justice to
keep up my mental state.
Without it I'm just an untied shoelace.
But my prayers were answered through God's grace.

You're not the only one who goes to
church so don't hate.

I bumped into this guy on the sidewalk
and I'll never
forget that date.
It was way back in July 17, 2028.
I knocked a guy down he looked like he
was somehow running away.

Syron: What are you some kind of thief, where are going anyway?

Running Man: "I'm going to the Subway."

Syron's Narration: He said in a nervous way.

Syron: You're lying, I can tell it by the way you shake.
Who are you and what are you doing out so late?

Running Man: "They call me Wheels and I'm just a car mechanic ok."
Not so fast I want you to prove it show me where your tools lay.

Wheels: "What are you a cop or somethin is that why you want to know where
I stay?"

Syron: Yeah, as a matter of fact street cop is the role I used to play.

Wheels: Fine I'll show you my place, then you'll believe what I have to say.

Syron's Narration: So we walk up to his little mechanic shop just before city gates.

And that's when I opened the door and saw
the suit that just blurts out crime doesn't pay.
No it didn't have a voice to express the things it had to say
but it has a crime fighting presence, it made the old police
uniform look like mere child's play.

So I asked Wheels about the suit he made
and why it had red and blue with a white stripe midway.

Wheels: "It's my prototype I'm going to sell it to some really rich guy if that's my fate."

Syron's Narration: Then I said that's my fate.

Wheels: "What do you mean that's my fate?"

Syron: I need that suit so I can meet my destiny date
and answer the desire in me I can't forsake.
The desire in my heart to fight crime won't go away.
It's a pain that stays from day to day, like a bad toothache.

Wheels: Alright ok.
You'll probably do more with it than some rich snob anyway.
But hey, just promise me this that one day you'll give back to my little mechanic shop so I can
live a quality life grade A
and I'll show you how that suit works

because the gadgets come in a wide array.

Syron's Narration: So from that place, right near city gate. On 7/17/28 is when I became the Syron and here I am today.

Me: Man that's awesome I guess I better tell you my story.

Syron: Don't worry I used my super sonic hearing
detecting decibels below 40.
I used sound to detect you before you could detect me.
Almost like you ignored me.

I listened to you talk to yourself and how you live life
for God's Glory.
Then I blasted by your window quicker than you could
turn your head to look for me.
But then I got low on thruster fluid and you gave me
ride , but yeah I already knew your story
cause it brought tears to my eyes like swimming pool chlorine.
Now keep heading east I have be dropped off by Wheels shop this morning.
Plus he can probably fix your time machine so you can
go back in time and stop your future from down pouring
storming, and then you go back to the year you were before me.

My Narration: So I drive the car and keep heading east.

I was killing 2 birds with one stone to
say the least.
Drop him off to where he needs to be
and I get to have my time machine put
together in one piece.

SSHHWWWOOOO!!!

I blast right by the jet in the air
with me.
He was making a right bank and he
almost hit me.
So I zoom around it for me and the
Syron's safety
because if I had stayed put that jet engine
would have ate me.

I keep cruisin above the clouds that look
so big and stately.
They remind me of the cotton that is
sown in the
shirts I've been wearin lately.
Dately, yes but I see more in plain shirts
than others
may see.

Call me crazy
but I'm driving a car right past, 1st class
and the passengers probably hate me
out of jealousy.

Syron: Land down there by city gate street.

Me: City gate street?
I thought when you said city gate it was
a real street B.
I thought they had wall around the city
with a real gate and city key, and gate
keep.

Syron: No way, it's just the name of the road that goes
around the city like the sewer creek.

My Narration: Then like a streak in the sky I made a sharp turn
to gate street.
I think the G forces may have made me a little weak.
We go straight, diving into city like hawk beak.
I slow down so we won't hit the trash heap
and we have a cool safe landing because I turn down the engine heat.

Riding slow on the road to get a relaxed feel
passing by banks and jewelry stores with glass windows
framed with steel
the Syron says buildings are made tougher so crooks
can't come in and steal.
Banks have to have 2 vaults to keep the money sealed.

Me: Hey Syron let's stop by the Fisherman's Pot to get a meal.

My Narration: So we walk into the seafood restaurant painted the
color teal
and we both eat the catch of the day that the fisherman
had reeled.

Then the waitress shows up in her high heels.

She was very beautiful but I could tell something was deceitful
about her appeal.
But the Syron kept looking at her like he was in love for real.
And I tapped him on the shoulder and said, "he who looks
upon another commits adultery" you go to church you know the deal.
Besides that woman has a look in her eye like she wants
to trip you up like a banana peel.

Syron: Alright, my bad, you're right, being with somebody like that
may be right to the feel.
But I know it will come back later to shock me like an electric eel.

My Narration: After he says that I see a big crowd swarm around
the Syron like a force field.

Crowd "Can I have your autograph," "can I have your autograph?"
They say as they guard the table like a shield
I pay for the tip then pay for the meal.
Then we scramble away from the crowd so we can go see Wheels.

Syron: How fast can this car go on the road?

Me: Like around 200 tops.

Syron: Well don't break the speed limit, I don't want you getting chased by the cops.

My Narration: So we keep rolling until he says stop.

Syron:	There, right there is Wheels shop. Right on gate road across the parking lot.
My Narration:	So we go in the garage and Wheels is like hey Pops.
Me:	Why did he call you Pops.
Syron:	Because under this suit I'm a 49 year old man but you can keep that on lock. Hey Wheels this is my friend, he picked me up when my fuel ran out of shock.
Wheels:	Wow kid, look at that car let me see what you got. Two jet engines and a big block. Man that Ford GT is hot.
Me:	Yeah it's nice and all but I need you to fix my time traveling clock.
Wheels:	No problem man, I'll take it to my welding room if you need me just knock.
Me:	Thanks Wheels, it means a lot.
Syron:	You know since I have my suit on I need to still check for crime around the block. Here kid put these put these jet shoes on we're gonna rock.
My Narration:	I got all my rocket fuel back, prepare to go above and beyond the flock.

WWHHISSHHH!!

We blast off on the spot.
Then the Syron starts pulling away with
some ridiculous

speeds over 600 knots.

Me: Slow down Syron we have to slowly
wipe the area with our eyes like a mop.

My Narration: So he slows down so we can get a good
look at the city plot.

Me: Hey look down there look at those
fighting dots.
Wait a minute those are people ganging
up on somebody
and they're punching his lights out like
rock em sock.

Syron: Look over there it's that woman from the
Fisherman's Pot she's sitting on the
ground waiting waving at me, to stop.

Me: But Syron we gotta save that guy before
he gets
dropped.

Syron: But the woman is in distress she wants
me to stop.

Me: No way she can wait, this guy is about to get
shipwrecked
and we better tow our boats over there
and dock.

Syron: Yeah if we're boats then I'm a land yacht.

SSHHPPHHOUUU!!

My Narration: The Syron blast down to the ground and save the guy he does not.
He's so attracted to that woman it keeps his judgment from flowing like a blood clot.
So he goes to save the damsel not in distress while I have to fight off thugs and risk being shot.

BBRRIISHHH! BOOM!

I come down on em like an atomic nuke.

1 of the Thugs: What are you the 82nd airborne troop?

Me: No I'm here to save that guy from the likes of you
before you beat his face in and make him turn blue.

1 of the Thugs: Well he owes us 7 Gs, plus an extra two and if you don't get out da way we'll do the same thing to you.

My Narration: Then one of em takes out a gun and it says

PWEW! PWEW! PWEW!

I duck, and I'm like "what is that, a laser gun that
must be something new."

1 of the Thugs: Naw man these things are mo than 10 years old year 2022.
But it don't make a difference no way cause we gone stomp you and make it look like an
accident like dog poo.

Me: Oh yeah well try telling that to my rocket shoe.

My Narration: I grab the victim and to the sky I blast off.

1 of the Thugs: Don't let him get away, shoot em

PWEW, PWEW, PWEW!

My Narration: One laser goes off by my head.
Another almost cuts through
but I keep flying straight up
to get away from the thug crew.

I ask the victim what his name is.
and he says his name is Andrew.

Me: Where should I drop you off Andrew?

Andrew: By the apartments downtown called Lakeview.
I will show you the way and I will lead you.
You saved my life back there how can I ever
thank you?

Me: Just tell me how you got into this trouble soup.

Those guys were kicking you around like beef stew.

Andrew: Well, I got a gambling problem and I don't know what to do.
I try to stop myself, but I can't resist the urge of roll, roll shoot.
I try to kick the habit but it still sticks to my back like glue.
Next thing I know somebody's beating me up over somebody else's loot.

My Narration: After he tells me about his problems I drop him
off by his apartment in Lakeview.
I sit him down on his couch and give him the truth.

Me: Look man, listen up Andrew.
I got a proposition for you and it's about a toll booth.
You don't like the road you travel on so why do you continue?
You say you don't like the traffic because it always
comes back to bite you
to fight you.
to psych you.
to smite you.
But despite all that you
don't get off the exit you just keep gambling right through
which is the same as paying a toll for a road that don't like you.

Andrew: Man, now that you told me that I don't know what to do.

Me: In your case it's not what you do it's when you need to alley oop.

But don't just toss your life up to any
who.
The ball's in your court but Jesus is the
one who died for you.

So why not pass the ball to the player
who
knows your every move.
He could tell ya which way the wind is
going
and what direction it blew.

I put Jesus on my team, and He turned
my life around
And I know He'll do the same for you.

Andrew: Man.
That's a hard choice to land.
Choosing Jesus is way harder than just to
going to the casino like I planned.

Me: In the Bible, it says repent ye for the Kingdom
of heaven is at hand.

Andrew: I know I feel stretched in 2 directions like a
rubber band.
Say a prayer with me so these bad habits
can be canned.
One day at a time I can be the man God
says I can.

Me: Let's say the prayer hold my hand.

Jesus, Jesus, Jesus that name so grand.
I ask that you come down and
show Andrew your will Lord show him
your plan
but not only show him the way, but let
him understand

what it means to be a true Christian and
take a stand.
Lord help him build his house on your
rock get him out of
the sand
so his house won't blow over like the
foolish man.

Lord you truly are God's sacrificial
lamb.
But in order for Andrew to be one of
yours
he has to be the salt and light so to God
he won't
taste bland.

God Savior, and God's favor, and Christ
blood
to wrap us up like saran.

Now I must end this prayer like it began.
In Jesus name we repent for the
Kingdom of heaven
is at hand.

Andrew: Thanks for praying with me now I
understand.
I want to make Jesus Lord and Savior so
I can follow God's plan.

Me: So surely God will bless you Andrew and
make you a new man.

My Narration:

ZZWWISSHHH!!!

I fly out of the building looking for the
Syron

cause no longer is gambling ruling over
Andrew's life like a tyrant.

But now he's saved and he can live for
Christ and
be strong as iron.
Now he has no beef with anybody like
chicken Tyson.

So now that he's alright I gotta go get the
Syron.
He was supposed to save the girl that trip
was only supposed to be a slight one.
Then he should have jetted over where I
was so he could have my fight won.
But he hadn't showed up yet.

He's still on fight one
with that girl from the Fisherman's Pot.
I bet she's a sly one.
I float down to the Fisherman's Pot
and I see no one, no Syron no waitress
not even a crumb.

I look around and everybody disappeared
like fog.
I'm guessin old Syron hopped out of here
with that girl like a frog.

I have no kind of communication with
him so I can't call.
I hope he's alright I probably better go to
Wheels'
shop and tell it all.

So I lift off the ground and don't bother
to crawl.
I soar through the air right over the
shopping mall.

I land in the mechanic's shop at Wheels' hall.
Then I knock knock knock on the door in the wall.
Wheels opens up the door and lets me in.

Me:	Is the Syron here yet it's almost 10?
My Narration	"Hmm I don't know where he is," he said rubbing his chin.
Wheels:	I thought he was with you out travelin hurling through the air like a javelin.
Me:	No he's not with me and I'm afraid he wondered into sin.
Wheels:	What do you mean?
Me:	Well he saw an attractive woman at the Fisherman's Pot and then we had to save this guy, but he left him to see that woman again. There's nothing wrong with seeing attractive women unless they lead you into sin. But as soon as the mind looks and desires then adultery's in the blend. But I'm worried about the Syron because he's a friend and think that woman is trying to use her grin to draw him in, and grab him by his fin and dirty him up like a pigpen. There's something bad about that woman, I just have that feelin. So I was trying to find you to find him

before she tricks him and uses him up
like an ink pen.

Wheels: I think we need to go over to my
laboratory pit.
That's where I made the costume and all
my other electronic tricks.

My Naration: Then the whole mechanic's shop flips
after he pulls the lever stick.
Then we're in some abyss
until he reaches over and flicks the light
switch
and then I see a real lab in the midst
of a mechanic shop and I didn't even
have to take a trip.
Then Wheels say "look at this toothpick"

Wheels: I'll break a piece off now look at it, it's
the size of a tick
and that's exactly the same size of the
tracking device I put on the Syron's
glove mitt.
We put it on so we could both get a grip.
We both know where each other's at all
times just in case trouble hits.

I'm looking at my scanner and it looks
like he's
not moving at all not even a lick
and his location is at the intersection of
Century
and Sixth.

Oh no!

Me: What?

Wheels: That's where the headquarters is for
Terramix.

Me: Who is Terramix?

Wheels: A big crime lord that runs all the illegal ships like clockwork.
He plans it all out like clockwork tick tock tick.

Me: Why do they call him Terramix?

Wheels: Cause when he shows up he adds terror to the mix.
If criminals came in a box he'd be the worse one in the kit.

But if you're gonna go after him you're gonna need this.
It's an exact copy of the Syron's costume.
Just like it every bit.

My Narration: So I put on the costume and make an exit.
I move through the air with a zoom.
I feel like I'm going so fast I'm going to break
the sonic boom.

I feel so light and aerodynamic in this costume.
It's tight but yet it has just enough room.
Man, I almost want to keep it and use it as a family
heirloom.
But I can't do that because I'm not a pickpocket goon.

Hey look at that building, it's so tall it's almost like it touches the moon

even though it's morning near the
afternoon.
Wait a minute that's that headquarters
Wheels said the Syron was marooned.

If that crime boss is bad as Wheels says
he is then I better get over there soon.
If Terramix gets a hold of him then he's
doomed

kicking the turbo up another step.
I got over to that building in a hurry
cause I pick up the pep.
Alright Syron I'm being you so I hope I
don't ruin your rep.

CRASH!!

I make more noise than a train wreck cause I bust through the sky scrapper window and I feel like I almost broke my neck.

Minion: "What was that sound?"

My Narration: Some guy says with a frown.

"Over here" I said as he turned around.

Minion: What, how did you get free we locked you in a cage that was laser bound.

Me: You didn't get the sticky note there's 2 Syrons now.

Minion: But B-B-B-B-B-But how?

My Narration: I grab him by his collar and said show me where the other Syron is now.

Minion: OW OW OW

I'll tell you if you just put me down.

Me: Ok so.

Minion: He's up the stairs in the upper room
highest one up off the ground.
If you're goin up there you have to watch out for the blood hounds.
Then you have to a find room that's completely round.
That's where the Syron's locked up and the Terramix hangs his crown
where he kicks his feet up lounging around.

Me: Thanks a lot man.

My Narration: And I blast all way to the stairs in a single bound.

Attack Dogs: RUFF RUFF!

My Narration: I see 10 dogs coming at me and I'm getting
ready to take em to the pound.
Two of the dogs knock me down and one of them
bit me on the toe.
Another one ran over and gnawed at my elbow.

These dogs were worse than I thought.
I better get out of this situation before
my trouble grows.

I press this button on my suit and it
makes
everything glow.
Then it starts popin off like a fireworks
show.
All the dogs get spooked and up stairs is
where
they go.
So I get up stairs slowly putting on the
the turbo.

I see the room and round is
understatement the
thing is shaped like a globe.
Over here somebody whispers in a voice
real low
and I tiptoe
to the edge of the room so the guards
won't know.
Then I see who was calling me and it
was the Syron himself
who spoke.
He was stuck in a cage with lasers that
can't be broke.

Syron: "Hey did Wheels send you or did you
come on your own?"

Me: Yeah wheels sent me, and he showed me
how to be your clone.
Now that I'm in this suit they probably
think I'm full grown.

My Narration: "You know I gotta get me of this cage" the
Syron groans.

Syron: I'm in a debtors prison and I didn't even take out a loan.

Me: Well how do I get you out of your little prison home?

Syron: Easy press the numbers 9-1-3-0 and you'll hear
a little tone.
That means the lasers are gone and I'm no longer caged like an animal but now I'm free to roam.

Me: So how did you get stuck in this place, you got
caught throwing some stones?

Syron: No kid, I didn't throw rocks and I didn't come alone.

Me: What do you mean?

Syron: Shhhh be quiet or they'll hear your voice like a metronome.
You gotta be silent as a lawn Nome.
I'll tell you everything, you just gotta listen to me like you got on headphones.

Instead of staying with you I went to save that woman that I sought.
I should have stayed with you and fought but instead I did wrong I didn't put others before myself like I ought.
And because of my wrong doing others had to pay the cost.

I left you lost. I left you in the cold like the frost

for a woman who wasn't mine, and at the
end I got double crossed.

She was almost like a devil with the
deception that she wrought.
She was so beautiful I couldn't detect her
evil with the
perception of my thoughts.
She told me to take her to a new room
that she bought.
I was too blinded by her beauty to realize
that it was the headquarters of a major
crime boss.

Soon as I walked in the door that's when
I got caught.
50 guards surrounded me, captured me,
and they were all
lead by the same woman that I brought.
And if I had only stayed true to the
lessons I was taught
I wouldn't have gotten deceived and
made to believe
such a tricky plot.
And they wouldn't have tied me up and
put me on laser
lock.

Waiting till 12 o'clock
when Terramix gave orders to take me to
the top.
Take my rockets out and then let me
drop
so that Terramix and the girl who threw
me for a trick
can watch me flop.
And they tell the police I ended my life
going for
hop.

But since you came there's still hope and we can still put their
iniquities to a stop.

Me: Alright I gotta plan but this is what we need.
I gotta put you back in the cage with the laser beam.
Let them tie you up and take your rockets off so they can drop you like chicken feed.

Syron: What are you saying, you sound like Terramix and his team.

Me: No man, I'm going to use my rockets save you from dropping to the ground like a seed.
I'm going to hide out until 12 o'clock when they start the lean mean
drop Syron to the to the ground machine.
We're gonna let them to believe they're finally gonna get rid of you like in their dreams.
Then I'm gonna pick you up, and close the book on em so the only thing they can read
is the serial number when they're incarcerated on their back behind their sleeve.

My Narration: So the Syron goes back in the cage with the laser.
And I hide in behind some boxes laying low like printing paper.
Then the clock strikes 12.

Terramix: It's time to meet your maker.
Ha ha ha I've made a fool of you Syron and my

girlfriend used you like a stapler.
I even let you think you were gonna take her. Now we're gonna take all the good you did and spoil it
and flush your life down the toilet like tissue paper.

My Narration: They take his rocket shoes of and take of his tracer.
Then they hook him to a crane and dangle him
off the top of the skyscraper.

Terramix: Any last words before your life dwindles down
to nothing like a used up eraser.

Syron: I give you your props if criminals had their own city you would be the mayor.
But at the end nobody gets away cause justice will hunt you down like Buffy the vampire slayer.

My Narration: The woman blows him kiss as the crane rotates
slowly like a conveyer.
The Syron drops and Terramix throws his girlfriend
Of the edge now I have to save her

SSHHHEEEEWWW!

I blast out of the boxes and like a jet fighter.

Then I leap over the edge like a scuba diver
and I grab the Syron in one arm and in the
other a harness comes out like a mountain hiker
and I use that to rope the woman in even though
I don't like her.
Then I shoot the top of the building
like a water geyser.

Terramix: What 2 Syrons and the girl I threw out like a lighter.
I'm sick of you justice goons I'm taking out my sniper.

POW POW!

My Narration: And I use the rockets to go even higher
then I come through the back of the building
and the guards seal us of like a diaper.

The Syron uses his costume to make a big
flash and it makes all the guards eyes hurt.
The Syron puts on his rocket shoes and plows through
all those guards like rain and he's the windshield wiper.
Stay here watch the girl I gotta take care of our little sniper.

Attractive Girl: I'm sorry, I am so so sorry,

Me: Calm down don't be so hyper.

Attractive Girl: But I was deceitful evil and cunning and subtle as a viper.

My Narration: She burst into tears, and I take out a tissue so she can wipe her
tears and I tell her to take of her scales and put on the right fur.

Attractive Girl: What do you mean put on the right fur?

Me: Listen carefully so you can decipher.

You were a snake that attracted people with your
scales.
Then you home in for the kill and watch them fail.
And you trap them with your jaws so they can't bail.
You found pleasure in devouring others
but you were only killing yourself slowly like a snail.
You caused discord with your lies and you
watched how others got impaled
but eventually your path of destruction became your own slime trail.

You say to me you don't have scales.
But the provocative clothing you used to cover yourself is what attracted men into your personal jail.

You say you don't have a slime trail
but everywhere you go people get condolence
cards in the mail.

You say you didn't cause anyone to be
impaled
but used your body to blind men as if all
they can read is brail.

You say you weren't killing yourself but
it was
only a matter of time before the tracks
you lay caught up to you, that's why
Terramix threw
you over the rail.

Your sin was not your beauty but how
you turned your beauty into scales.
But if you would just used your beauty
for fur
you could help other people and use your
gentleness to heal their hurt.

You should fully clothe yourself so
won't cause
men to deter.
If you have fur
no longer will you be the snake
and make peoples lives worse.
But if you put away your scales you
could take
the pain away like the school nurse
put on Christ and let gentleness cover
you like fur
so your father in heaven can say I am
well pleased with her.

My Narration: The woman continues to cry and I give
her a hug.
I can tell she felt bad about what she did
so I embraced her with love.

What's your name I asked she said,

"Marie" she said peaceful as a dove.
Thank you she said as she gave me a gentle back rub.

Meanwhile the Syron is fighting
Terramix and he has
his hands full.

POW POW POW!

Syron dodges every bullet Terramix sniper riffle pulls.
Then the Syron comes down and snatches the gun
and breaks it over his knee once he sees the barrels not full/

Then Syron says "no weapons no rockets let's duel."
Terramix reaches over and throws a box of fuel.
Syron ducks underneath and kicks him in the face
like a mule.

Terramix punches him saying "Who dares to fight me?"
"Dare to challenge me who will?"
Terramix picks Syron up the Syron and throws him into the wall.
"You are truly a fool if you will."
Tackling Terramix to the floor, he says "I will challenge
you and your ways so cruel."
The punches go back and forth until the Syron hits him
with an upper cut and says justice is what I will.

Terramix falls to the ground in defeat
Syron beats
him in the duel while keeping his his
rocket shoes still on his feet.
Then the police swarm in and arrest
Terramix
in all of his conceit.

Chief of Police: You're a good man Syron, we want to give you one of these.

My Narration: And the chief gives him a badge just like the
one on the real police.
I take off my costume because I have my
regular clothes underneath.
So all the officers, I myself can meet.
Then Marie
goes up to the cops just to be friendly
and greet.
Then they ask the Syron and me "should
we arrest
her too or should we leave?"
He says "let her go, because she's a
changed woman in deed."

Chief of Police: Ok Officer Syron she is free.
And your partner here, we give you this
metal
of honor, because the truth you tell is
what people need.

Me: Thank you, thank you for all that you've given me.

Chief of Police: And I hope you officers continue to stop
criminals
like Terramix that will do anything for
greed.

BBBRRSHHEEEEWW!

My Narration: Me and Syron take off to see Wheels with great speed.
We stop by the garage to tell Wheels about how we made a scene
and how Terramix was going to prop the Syron
a quarter before 12:15
and the girl that went nice after she used to be mean
and how the Syron took down Terramix and his whole regime

Wheels: I always knew you could do it welcome to the team.

Me: Yeah man I would but you know this year is just not my stream.
So I gotta rise up and out like the boiling pot of steam.
I gotta go back in 2007 cause I'm still 16.

So, Wheels, Syron its been real
but I gotta close the glass door to this alternate reality and go back to my screen.

Wheels: Yeah um, about that screen and your plot to get back to reality scene.
What I'm about to say might make you scream.
I wasn't able to fix the past button on the time machine.

My Narration: I let out big sigh and say I guess I have to take a risk that involves
me going to the future self to see if the technology evolves
and my future self telling me now the time machine revolves.
So I get in my Ford GT and do a tire stall.

Me: Piece out my brothers I'll never forget y'all.

My Narration: After I say my good bye I burn out of the garage with a mystery to solve.

PART VI

My Narration:

So now I driving around trying to figure
out what my
future self might be telling me. By then
man I might be a celebrity
or a composer synthesizing some type of
melody
or I might be an entrepreneur in charge
of magazine Ebony.
But I hope I'm not foolish enough to
buy everything somebody's selling me
or become bankrupt, or worse commit a
felony
or make a bad mistake and somebody
tell on me.
But I guess the only way to know is to
go to
future and find out whether I'm still on Earth
or at the pearly gates so heavenly.

I fly up and put the jets on and go
forward to the year 2070.
And in a flash I travel to my future just
to look for a past.
If this plan doesn't work then 2007
won't be a button I could mash.
I would be gone from my own time
forever never to go back
sucked up from normality and out of the
steady flow of the time space continuum
like a Hoover vac.
I don't know if I can take that.

A situation like this how can I be laid
back.
Even if someone gave me new Maybach

I don't think I could sleep without taking
a fake nap.

I need to find my future self so I can get
out of here ASAP.
If there was a bus that stopped off at
different years
than I would take that.

I still got the 30 million dollars from the
museum that I got paid at.
But now I'm at the point where I'm
ready to pay it all back.
That would be great in fact.
If that's all I had to do to get to my own
year and state in fact
I would do that except life is not as easy
as a piece of cake
in fact. Life right now is more like the
residue from the cake which is plaque.
But like the dentist God is, by His might
I might be taken back
to before I even set foot in a time
machine and the cake was even cut in
half.

So I cruise along in the dark night sky.
Then below me I see a pulsating bright
light.
So I float down to the ground like an
unwounded kite would fly.
It could be an emergency situation so I
can't just drive by.
So I need to go attempt to help them like
the good Samaritan might try.

So I make a smooth landing with the jets
on shy.

I turn the engine off to see what's going on cause I don't see
a light in my eye.
I step out of the car and all I see is a rocky desert
and an old guy.

Old Man: I knew you'd come down you always tried to be as sweet as apple pie.

My Narration: But the old man didn't look stranded or in need of care.
So I'm thinking that light was a lie.

Me: Hey you're not a person in need you're just a phony.

Old Man: I'm only a phony if you're a phony.
What you put on yourself goes on me.

Me: What are you talking about old homie?

Old Man: For one I'm lonely.
If friendship was muscle I would be bony.
I would be only skin deep with all bone and no meat. My heart is stony
because I watch all of my friends die and it seems
like everyday I have to get new cronies.

I feel like every time I get a new sound system somebody breaks my Sony.
I watch generations, and generations of horses grow old and give birth to new ponies.
But at the end of the day it seems like this whole
Earth life is phony

knowing that what you put on yourself
goes on me.

Me: What are you talking about why do you keep saying that phrase?

Old Man: You mean you haven't figured it out all ready, a young mind at your age.
I'm your future self in your later days.
Oh, that's why you keep saying that phrase.

My Future Self: Yes, and that phrase what keeps me free, and in a cage.
Free because I am not bound by the foolishness that comes my way.
Yet in a cage because for the foolishness that was already done
I still have to pay.
Take away the time machine and I'm free to break away.
But add it to me and it's a cage for the foolishness
already done and I still have to pay.

Me: You mean take back the 30 million dollars is that what you mean by pay.

My Future Self: No, but you will have to do that, but that's not what I mean by pay.
Time is money that's what they used to say.
Well then money is time that's what I say today.
Because all the money in the world couldn't compensate
for all the years on Earth I lay
trying to find the time machine
technology to get me back in
the past to the real year I stay.

I have to keep skipping ahead in time so
I don't die in the future
or get old and gray.

But time has still caught up with me
anyway.
Looking for a time machine, while
watching a kid play
nobody has the technology so I skip
ahead another 50 years
and it's the kid's funeral the very next
day.

Try doing that again 10 times if you may.
Then finding your mom, dad, and brother
died in between the years of time that
you skipped away.
Going through stuff like that will put
your mind in a craze
in a maze
in a stupid daze
in a stupid faze
chanting a stupid phrase.

What you put on you goes on me, the
foolishness that you do today
is the foolishness that tomorrow has to
pay.
But in all the stuff I went through the
only thing that got me out was God's
praise.

Went through 500 years and I'm only 80
years of age.
Year 2570 and in my quest for time I
found someone to help aid.

Monna Merrit created a time machine
that can go to the past
so I could come back to this year and
now I'm saved.
Now I feel refreshed like somebody gave
me a glass of lemonade
cause God answered all of my prayers
that I prayed.

But it's not fair
that you can skip back and forth through
time
while other people have to live with the
problems that they bare.
Plus, man is not meant travel up and
down chronological steps
because that's in conflict with God's up
only time stairs.
Unless you're in God's Kingdom which
is eternal, there is no time there.
But if you're playing the Earth game you
can only go forward just like
every other player.

So we're going to erase everything you
ever did with the all the time
machines that can fly in the air
and the other time machine that in your
mind you might share.
Everything you did for yourself will be
erased, all 30 million dollars
and you won't keep a dime.
The little girl you killed will still be
alive, she will be just fine.
All of those historical figures you froze
will be brought to their own time.

Every grain of dirt you may have
encountered, all the filth and the grime

will all be washed away, like green
slime.
No longer will you go in and out of the
time line.

My words that I am telling you probably
taste sour like lemon lime.
But you can't go around ruling the
universe like a star
with a car that travels through time.

While others have to work hard to shine
you can't just hop in the future when to
everyone else
has to wait for the future because to the
future they're blind.

But what you and a lot of other people
don't realize is the future is just the
leftovers of today's meals you dine.
If you want tomorrow to be nice to you
then to today you have to be kind.

You can't expect to just jump up and be
happy later if right now all you do is
whine.
So if you want people to stop at the end
of your road the next
day, then today you have to put up a stop
sign.
The time space continuum is not just for
Einstein.
You have to go forward in time and only
remember not to look behind.

If you want an apex later in life then
today
you have to build up to your prime.
If you want your pencil sharpened the
next minute

then this second you have grab the
sharpener and grind.
If you want to go to the top of the ladder
then today you have to climb.

You can't just step in your time machine
to solve your struggles.
Just fast forward and rewind.
You have to go on and earn something in
life only then
can you say it's mine.
Anybody can wish for a time machine
and just transport to the hope they find.

But it takes a real man to except reality
and except the fact that the only future is
in the mind.
And the allowance from today to become
yesterday
is truly divine.
All we can do is prepare for tomorrow
today
and pray to God He grant us the time.

Have a vision in your heart, because
without vision the people parish
like old candy at Valentine's.
A vision for the future is what keeps the
present from
blowing us around like wind chimes.

But to actually go through mess with
time violates
God's order of events that he a lined.
But for your situation all that you learned
needs to stick to your brain like quills
from a porcupine.

So I'm going to knock you out with a frying pan
and send you back to your own time.
But fear not, because all the knowledge you gained from
this experience won't come to a decline.

When you wake up you'll think it was all a dream, but you'll
want to write about it in a book called Future Rebuke and the whole
thing will rhyme.

So other people can learn from your experience, especially the
people you told about Jesus over their lifetime.
But I need to write note on your TV that says don't watch channel 9
because if you get the time machine out of the movie you'll ruin
your life and mine.

BANG!!!

My Narration: My future self hits me with a frying pan and it felt like my head hit a land mine.

PART VII

Me:

Man, I had this crazy dream, and it made
me want to get out of bed and scream.
It started out with this weird rhythmic
rhyming scheme.

Today we are talking to boundaries and
telling them to move.
On paper I'm not bound by time space or
any other issues.
So after acquiring all of this new
knowledge this is what we gone do.
I'm going to talk to my future self for a
future rebuke.

But I say let's start right here right now
in 2007.
I'm age 16 and I'm in the present.
Today I'm on my way to heaven.
But I need to make sure I got God in
2011.

References

Matthew 7:26
(foolish man, house on the sand)

The book of Job
(who are you to contend with the almighty) concept

Matthew 5:5
(meek shall inherit the earth)

Matthew 3:2 and 4:17
(repent for the Kingdom of heaven is at hand)

Matthew 5:13-16
(salt and light)

Matthew 5:28
(whoever looks upon another commits adultery)

II Peter 3:8
(a thousand years is like a day I see)

James 4:14
(your life is like a vapor to me)

Psalm 23
(lie down in green pastures)

2Corinthians 5:7
(live faith, not by sight)

Joseph Conrad's Heart of Darkness

(the horror the horror)

Terminator
(I'll be back)

Note: slang terminologies represented in book "B"and "par" are not derogatory terms or abbreviations they are just simple pronouns used to describe and address individuals

Note: though Edward Thomas Tookes was the author,God had a huge helping handThroughout the entirety of this project

Made in the USA
Lexington, KY
21 September 2011